Witch Twins
and the
Ghost of Glenn Bly

ADELE GRIFFIN
Witch Twins
and the
Ghost of Glenn Bly

ILLUSTRATIONS BY

Jacqueline Rogers

HYPERION PAPERBACKS FOR CHILDREN

NEW YORK

Text copyright © 2004 by Adele Griffin

Illustrations copyright © 2004 by Jacqueline Rogers

All rights reserved. No part of this book may be reproduced or transmitted in any form or by any means, electronic or mechanical, including photocopying, recording, or by any information storage and retrieval system, without written permission from the publisher. For information address Hyperion Books for Children, 114 Fifth Avenue, New York, New York 10011-5690.

Printed in the United States of America

First Hyperion Paperback edition, 2005

1 3 5 7 9 10 8 6 4 2

Library of Congress Cataloging-in-Publication Data on file.

ISBN 0-7868-1941-3 (tr.)

ISBN 0-7868-5496-0 (pbk.)

Visit www.hyperionbooksforchildren.com

For Kate and Lizzie

Contents

1

The Real Exciting News

THE BABY HAD A FAT FACE and was bald. He was not very cute. In fact, Luna Bundkin thought he looked like a toad.

She shook her head at her identical twin sister, Claire, who was cradling the baby in her arms.

"Little toady!" Luna whispered.

"Little Tony?" Their father, Louis Bundkin, scratched his head, thinking. "Hmm. Tony is a nice name. But I think we will stick with Bert."

"Can I give Bert back to you now?" Claire asked their stepmother, Fluffy, who was sitting in her hospital bed. "My arms are tired."

"Wait! First let me hold him," said Justin.

Claire handed baby Bert to Justin. Luna kept her own hands clasped behind her back. She stepped closer to their mother. She did not want to hold Bert. He looked like he might do something loud or smelly or gloppy.

"Thanks, ya'll, for coming to visit us," said Fluffy. "Bert is a whole lotta lucky to have twin half sisters and a half brother in his family!"

"Kitchy, kitchy," cooed Justin. "Hey, Bert. Hey, little guy!"

"Um, isn't it time to go?" asked Luna. "Doesn't this place close for business soon?"

"Luna, we're not in a restaurant. We're in a hospital!" Claire rolled her eyes at her twin.

"It is almost eight o'clock," said Jill Bundkin. "I'm sure Fluffy and Bert want to rest. Let's get going, kids. Good night, everybody."

They exchanged hugs and said good-byes. Then Luna, Claire, Justin, and their mother trooped out of the hospital and into the drab November night. Their mother whistled between her teeth. "Taxi!" she yelled. Immediately, a cab screeched to the curb.

"Did any of us look like toads when we were born, Mom?" asked Luna as they taxied down the streets of Philadelphia, heading back to their town house at 22 Locust Street.

"Oh, Bert will improve," said their mother. "He just needs to fill out."

"He needs more hair, too," added Claire.

"Mom, are you sad?" asked Justin as they walked up the steps to their front door. "You know, since Dad has a new family with his new wife, and all?"

"No, I'm not sad. I don't need any more children than you wonderful three," answered their mother. "Anyway, life is always an interesting mix of surprises. Bittersweet, I'd call it."

"Like, if you and Dad didn't *bitterly* divorce, he never would have met *sweet* Fluffy, and you never would have met *sweet* Steve?" asked Luna.

"Well . . . that's not exactly what I meant,"

said their mother as she unlocked the door. "But definitely, you three kids are the sweetest things in my life. And Steve is very sweet, too."

Steve was their mother's boyfriend. He was a chef. Right now he was using the Bundkins' kitchen to create his newest food experiment, hot chocolate–cauliflower soup. (When Steve made his own kitchen too messy, he used the kitchen at 22 Locust.)

"I smell something bittersweet!" Claire sniffed the air as they walked into the front hall.

"The gang's all here!" called Steve from the kitchen.

"The gang" turned out to be Grandy and Grampy, who were plunked at the table slurping up large bowls of Steve's soup.

"Mom and Dad! What a surprise. I didn't see your car out front." Their mother looked mystified. "How did you get here?"

"Oh, we were in the neighborhood," said Grandy.

"But *why* are we in the neighborhood, Arianna? We live twenty-five miles away!"

grumbled Grampy. "Oh me, oh my. My memory's on the blink again. I must be getting old."

Luna and Claire exchanged smiles. They knew Grampy's bad memory was not to blame. The reason that their grandparents were in the neighborhood was because Grandy was a five-star witch, and she had secretly instaported herself and Grampy from their home in Bramblewine straight to Philadelphia. Grandy usually cast this spell during rush hour, because she hated traffic.

The twins knew about the instaport spell because they were witches, too. In fact, Grandy, Luna, and Claire were the only witches in the whole family. Nobody—not even the twins' own parents—had any idea about this huge, important secret.

"It doesn't matter *how* we got here," said Grandy. "The reason we are here is to share some exciting news."

"More exciting than our half brother, Bert Bundkin?" asked Justin.

"*I* think so," Grandy answered in a huff. "But

I don't like brand-new babies. They all look like toads. Tell them the *real* exciting news, Fred."

"The *real* exciting news," announced Grampy, "is that next week, your grandmother and I have been invited to play golf at the Seniors Silver Loch tournament in Scotland."

"Oh, wow, that's great," chorused everyone in not-very-excited voices.

"And we're taking our three fabulous grand-children," said Grandy.

"OH WOW! THAT'S GREAT!" yelled Luna and Claire in very-very-excited voices. "Scotland! Scotland!"

Justin looked upset. "But I can't go to Scotland," he said. "Next week is Thanks-giving. That's the team's most important football weekend ever, and I'm a running back. Sorry, Grandy and Grampy. I can't let the guys down. You'll have to count me out."

The twins went silent, feeling sorry for Justin. Then they started jumping around again and yelling, "Scotland! Scotland!"

Their mother leaned against the kitchen

counter and put on her most serious face. Jill Bundkin was a doctor, and she knew how to make a serious face if she needed one.

"Even if you only took the twins, this is still a very expensive trip, folks, don't you think?" she asked.

"Not really. We can pay for tickets with our frequent-flier miles, and we get to stay for free at a Scottish castle," Grandy explained.

Grampy frowned. "Which just happens to be run by Arianna's old flame, Mac."

"Oh, hush, Fred," snapped Grandy. "I married you, not him, didn't I?"

"A castle?" Luna squealed. She had never heard of anything so romantic. "With gardens and moats and tea at half past four in the drawing room?"

"Absolutely, Luna, dear," assured Grandy.

"It's creaky and leaky," said Grampy. "We'd be better off at the Holiday Inn."

"Mac's castle, Glenn Bly, is one thousand years old," said Grandy. "It's quite spectacular. There's even a stable of horses to ride."

"It's not *his* castle," grumped Grampy. "He had to sell it. He's only the curator."

Luna put her hand to her heart. Although she had never been horseback riding before, she was sure she would love-love-love it. To live for a week in a castle and go horseback riding was a dream come true. As long as the horse didn't go too fast.

Justin's mouth twitched in suspicion. "Wait a minute! Isn't Scotland where they make boys wear those plaid skirts?"

"Tartan kilts," Grampy corrected.

"Isn't Scotland where they make you eat those dry crackers?" asked Claire.

"You mean shortbread," said Grandy. "It's yummy."

"And doesn't a monster live in some lake in Scotland?" asked Justin.

"The Loch Ness monster," said Grampy. "Her name is Nessie, but nobody has seen her for years. She keeps to herself."

"It'll be Thanksgiving week, but the twins would still miss two and a half days of school," said their mother, running a hand through her hair so that it spiked up like a toothbrush.

"Oh, phooey. What's a couple of days?" coaxed Grandy. "And with Justin playing football, that leaves you and Steve lots of time without kids underfoot."

Luna could tell from her mother's eyes that this was an interesting thought.

Now Steve held up a dripping ladle. "Who else wants to test my soup?" he asked.

"Not me," said Luna politely.

"Not me," said Claire, less politely.

"I'll try it!" said Justin, who was growing an inch a month and always on the lookout for extra food. But Luna and her sister knew better. Steve's recipes needed lots and lots of practice to be perfect.

The twins sprang upstairs to their bedroom, where they squeezed onto the one desk chair, turned on their computer, and logged online to check out a few Web sites about Scotland.

"I wish we had a coat of arms like a real Scottish family," said Luna.

"I wish we had bonny blue eyes and curly ginger hair, like True Scottish Lasses," said Claire.

Luna shrugged. She preferred having brown eyes and matching-colored hair. She liked to match, period. Claire did not mind messes and guesses, but Luna treasured tidiness. It was just one of the ways that the twins were as different on the inside as popcorn was from cornflakes.

There was a knock on the door, and then Grandy peeked her head through. "Girls, I want a witch-word with you," she said.

Immediately, the twins bounced to attention. A witch-word was no joke.

Grandy slipped into their room and shut the door, then set her ear against it to check that Justin was not eavesdropping.

"Our trip to Scotland is not all fun and games, young witches mine," whispered Grandy. "Golf is the *official* reason. But anyone who has seen your grandfather and me play knows we are awful golfers. In fact, I had to use a three-star spell to snag us an invitation to this tournament. It's very exclusive."

"Isn't that called cheating?" asked Luna.

"No, it's called an emergency," Grandy answered, "because there is also an *unofficial* reason we are going to Scotland. And that is to help Mac. He wrote me an e-mail explaining that he is having a problem with ghosts." She patted her hair. "Helping him out is the least I can do. I broke Mac's heart when I ran off with your grandfather, you know."

"Why are you taking Luna and me along?" asked Claire.

"To watch and learn, obviously," Grandy answered. "Every witch needs to know how to pop a ghost."

"'Pop a ghost'?" Luna shivered. "That sounds gross."

"It's the only way to handle them. Ghosts are pesky. Plus, they'll complain your ear off if you give 'em half a chance."

"How does Mac know that you're a ghost-popping expert?" asked Claire. "Isn't that a secret, witch-y skill?"

"Of course." Grandy blushed. "But back when I was young and foolish, I might have bragged a little, teeny bit about my skills with popping and summoning ghosts. I was a bit surprised myself that Mac remembered. Then again, everything about me is hard to forget. Now, girls, are you helping or not?"

"Five-star witch Arianna of Bramblewine," said Claire, excitedly, "as a one-and-a-half-star apprentice witch, I offer my service!"

"Me, too," squeaked Luna.

"Thanks, girls. I knew I could count on you." Then Grandy clapped her hands together and instaported herself back down to the kitchen.

"Gosh," said Claire after Grandy had gone. "I never met a ghost before. This'll be fun!"

"Fun? Fun? I don't want to meet any ghosts!" exclaimed Luna. "And I especially don't want to pop any! Ick!"

"Oh, Loon, don't be a doomsday prophet," chided Claire.

But Luna knew that she had a point. Never in her life had she caught sight of a spirit or a glimpse of a ghost, or a peek at a phantom.

Now, the idea that she'd soon be meeting up with a real, castle-haunting, Scottish spookster made her scalp prickle and her toes curl.

2
Daphne Bly, T.S.L.

CLAIRE HATE-HATE-HATED the cold. She was glad to leave behind a drab November in Philly for the green lands and blue skies of Scotland. She'd downloaded a lot of pictures of Scotland, and the weather looked divine.

So Claire was shocked when she stepped off the plane at Inverness Airport to discover that it was gray and cold and very, very damp.

"Hey! Where's the sun?" Claire frowned up at the sky. "Where are all the sheep and grass like what I saw on those Scotland Web sites?"

"Don't be a nincompoop," snapped Grandy, toggling up her overcoat. "Scotland in November is just like Philadelphia in November, only Scotland has more rain. Oh, what a nice, cloudy day! I hope you packed snuggly clothes."

Claire didn't answer. Suitcase-packing was a chore and a bore, and she had waited until the last minute to do it. Her swimsuit, cutoff shorts, Camp Bliss T-shirt, and wraparound movie-star sunglasses weren't exactly *snuggly*. In fact, the warmest clothes Claire had with her were the jeans, purple sweater, and rainbow-sleeved parka that she was wearing now.

But she forgot about all that when she looked again at her stiff new passport with its first stamp ever.

As they entered the airport lobby, a jolly airline employee waved to them.

"Ta! Enjoy your holiday!"

Ta! Claire had never heard that expression before. It sounded very Scottish.

"Fred! Arianna!" In the Arrivals section of

the airport lobby, a short, plump man in a tweed cap waved from behind the ropes.

"Why, it's Mac!" Grandy leaped ahead, leaving Claire and Luna to trundle behind dragging the carry-on luggage. Grampy took up the rear and walked the slowest.

"Cheerio! I'm Michael MacCorckle Bly, otherwise known as Mac!" Grandy's old flame spoke with a Scottish brogue. His bright blue eyes were like two chips of the Scottish sky Claire had been hoping to see. "You must be Claire and Luna!" he said. "But how will I know which from the other?"

"I talk more," Claire offered helpfully. That was what kids at the twins' school, Tower Hill Middle, always said—although she herself didn't really believe it.

Mac laughed and led the way to the Baggage Claim.

"Ta! All the cars' steering wheels are on the wrong side," observed Claire after they had picked up their bags and started for the parking lot. As of five minutes ago, *ta* was

Claire's new favorite word.

"Yes, yes," said Mac. "You see, here in Scotland, our steering wheel is on the wrong side. Or, as we call it, the right side. But not to worry! It's all quite safe."

Claire bounced in her shoes as she climbed into Mac's compact green minivan. Scotland! Then she glanced at Luna, who looked scared. Claire guessed it was on account of the wrong-sided, right-sided steering wheel. Poor Luna got nervous about the very same things that seemed cool to Claire.

During the winding drive to Glenn Bly, Claire kept her gaze fixed out the window so that she could shout out what she saw along the way.

"There's a funny red phone booth! Ta, I see some goats! I see a moss-covered bridge! Now I'm looking at a sign for a *petrol* station. *Petrol* means gasoline. Ta! I spy teensy-weeny purple flowers!"

"My, my," Mac remarked. "You are very observant, Claire. But actually, '*ta*' is the Scottish word for 'thank you'."

"Is *observant* the Scottish word for annoying?" asked Luna.

"Shut up, Loony-goon," Claire answered.

"Why don't you shut up, stinky-ugly?" asked Luna.

"Why don't you shut up, creepy-icky?" Claire retorted. "You are already making my Scottish highland adventure bittersweet."

"If both you girls don't hush," said Grandy, twisting around on the front seat, "I'm going to feed you toes first to Scotland's famous fang-toothed, water-dwelling barge rats."

For a while, the twins kept silent.

"There it is!" squeaked Luna. She tapped the window glass. "The castle!"

"Good eyes, Luna," said Mac.

Claire's head snapped around. No fair! She had wanted to spot the castle first! She stared. Up in the distance, Glenn Bly rose in a splendor of stone walls and towers.

"Crenellated," said Grampy, "is the name for the special jagged cut along the roof."

Crenellated—what a word! It reminded

Claire of the sound of teeth crunching into a buttered English muffin.

Mac turned through the castle's open iron gates and slowed the van so that everyone could enjoy the sight of the castle's surrounding fields and woodland.

"'Glenn Bly Welcomes You.'" Claire read the hinged sign that swung from a post. "I see the horse stable! I spy a watchtower!"

"Mac, it's just as beautiful as I remembered," said Grandy as they parked behind the castle and piled out of the van. "You must be running a profitable bed-and-breakfast business."

"I don't see any guests," grumped Grampy.

"Aye. November is a slow time for tourists." Mac cleared his throat and, in a louder voice, called, "That's why young Daphne will be glad for a bit of company. Right-o, Daphne?"

"Daphne?" repeated Claire. She looked around. All she saw was brown lawn bordered by green pines. "Who's Daphne? Where is she? Does *young* mean she's older than eleven or younger than eleven?" The twins had celebrated their birthdays last month, on Halloween. Claire was happy to be eleven, finally!

"Daphne is my granddaughter. She is ten," answered Mac.

Now Claire's ears picked up a rustle. She looked up-up-up into the branches of the ever-greens. She could not spy anyone.

"Who goes there?" Claire shouted.

"I go here! And I'm turning eleven in two days!" said a voice from above.

"Daphne, not too high," warned Mac. "Daphne's a bit untamed," he explained. "Right-o. I expect everyone could use some refreshment."

With a hand at Grandy's elbow, Mac led them all around to the front of the castle and through its iron-hinged front doors.

The inside front hall of Glenn Bly was larger than Tower Hill Middle's lunchroom cafeteria.

"Crumbs! You could do ten backflips in a row across this floor!" Claire exclaimed, hoping someone would invite her to try.

"Look!" Luna shrieked, and everybody jumped. She pointed. "A hanging tapestry, a stone fireplace, and a curving staircase! How castle-ish!"

"Er, yes," said Mac. "The drawing room is this way. I've set out an early supper."

Claire walked across the flagstones to get a better look at the large, faded tapestry.

"That tapestry depicts the Battle of Sodden Field, a bloody combat that took place in 1616," Mac explained. "The Boyds against the Blys. Needless to say, the Blys won, otherwise this castle would be called Glenn Boyd, and I wouldn't be standing here. But victory came at a cost. Nearly four hundred soldiers were lost."

"Ah, for shame," clucked Grampy.

Claire scanned the soldiers that had been stitched into the tapestry. Immediately, her eye caught the face of a young man who did not look much older than her brother, Justin. Dressed in plain chain-mail armor and astride a silver steed, the boy and his horse seemed to glow from the fabric. In fact, Claire thought, they looked alive enough to charge straight off the tapestry and gallop through the castle doors.

Claire sniffed. If she hadn't known any

better, she would have sworn she smelled strawberries.

Transfixed, Claire kept her eyes on the tapestry boy, even after the others drifted out of the
hall and into the drawing room.

"That's Sir Percival Quilty," said a voice at
her shoulder. "He was a brave young knight who
died in battle."

Claire turned. A girl stood next to her. She
was taller than Claire and blue-eyed like Mac.
Her curly ginger hair was scattered with ever-
green needles, and there was a sly look on her
face.

A True Scottish Lass!

"I am Daphne Bly of the castle Glenn Bly,"
said the girl.

"And *I* am Claire Bundkin of the United
States of America," answered Claire.

"Well, American Claire, I'm glad you think
you're brave enough to stay with us here," said
Daphne Bly, "considering that our castle is
haunted by a fierce and beastly ogre."

Claire wasn't scared that easily. "I've heard

you had a haunting problem. But can you prove it?" she dared.

Daphne looked surprised. Then unsure. Then determined. "Yes!" she declared, flushing. "Just not this minute."

"Sorry, lass. Seeing is believing!" said Claire.

Nose in the air, Daphne flipped around and skipped off to join the others.

"Aha!" Mac smiled as Claire followed Daphne into the drawing room. "Here is my granddaughter. Daphne, may I introduce you to the lovely Mrs. Arianna Bramblewine; her short and balding husband, Fred; and their twin granddaughters, Claire and Luna Bundkin."

Without a look in Claire's direction, Daphne said hello and shook hands nicely with everyone. Then she popped a biscuit into her pocket, turned on her heel, and trotted out the door as fast as she had entered.

"I do apologize," said Mac, looking somewhat embarrassed. "Daphne doesn't have much practice meeting people. As you might remember, Arianna, dear, my granddaughter is an orphan.

She's been my ward ever since she was but a wee thing of six months, when her parents died in a terrible hang-gliding accident. I'm afraid Daphne's been left to herself too much."

"Ooh. An orphan raised in a castle. How romantic," whispered Luna.

Claire frowned. She didn't think that girl was one bit romantic.

On the contrary, Daphne Bly, True Scottish Lass, had Claire's witch senses pricked up for mischief.

3
Bold Night, Shy Knight

FROM THE BEDROOM window, Luna watched a pale vein of lightning split the night sky. She closed her eyes and snuggled deeper into the feather mattress, counting *one-crackled-cauldron, two-crackled-cauldron, three—*

Crrr—aaack! Ka-boom! Blam!

"Claire?" she whispered. "Are you awake?"

"Of course I'm awake!" Claire's voice came from the other side of the canopy bed they shared. "Who could sleep through this lightning and thunder?"

"Not me. I wish our room was cozy," said Luna, although earlier that evening, she had been delighted when Mac had shown the girls to this beautiful bedroom. It had its own Juliet balcony, corner harpsichord, and a romantic name, Elderberry Chamber.

With their grandparents down the hall and settled into the even more majestic Peacock Chamber, they had all turned in for an early sleep.

But there'd be no sleep in this earsplitting storm.

Ka-boom!

"Crikey!" Luna shifted up in the bed. She did not like unexpected noises. "Claire! I just had a spooky thought! Do you think Glenn Bly's ghost scared up this storm?"

"If a ghost scared up this storm, he's doing a fantastic job!" Claire sat up, too, and squinted at her sister. "Loon, why are you wearing your lady-in-waiting Princess and the Pea costume as a nightgown?"

Luna touched the lace neckline. "Because I love-love-love olden-days clothes," she said. "And this was the most romantic thing I had." She squinted back at her sister. "Claire, why are you wearing your Camp Bliss T-shirt to bed? Aren't you cold?"

"No. I love-love-love this T-shirt," said Claire.

Kerrr-blam!

"Ugh!" Luna covered her ears.

But Claire's nostrils flared. "Luna! I smell strawberries! Can you?"

Luna sniffed and shook her head no. Her sense of smell was not good. She tilted her head toward the door. "But I do hear a *jingle-jingle, clinkity-clink*. It's very soft. Do you hear it?"

"No," said Claire. "But if I use my nose and you use your ears, maybe we can figure out what's going on. Come on, Luna. Time for some detectiving!"

With that, Claire leaped out of the bed. Luna noticed that her twin was also wearing a pair of cutoff jeans shorts. Claire definitely had forgotten to pack her nightgown. Probably her toothbrush and her spy globe, too. Crumbs! Claire was a bad suitcase-packer!

Luna slid out of the bed, knotted on her bathrobe, and slid on her pink fuzzy slippers. "Proceed with caution!" she reminded her sister. Luna never thought that Claire proceeded with enough caution.

Barefoot and bathrobeless, Claire slipped out the bedroom door.

In the echoing corridor, they could hear rain loud as marching drums against the roof and stone walls. The hallway's narrow windows gave a view of moonlit trees bent backward against the wind.

Luna shivered as she tiptoed behind her sister. The ghost of Glenn Bly must be very angry to cast such a spooky storm!

As they moved down the hallway, the *jingle-jingle, clinkity-clink* noises got louder.

"My nose will lead the way!" Claire whispered.

Luna hooked Claire's pinkie through her own to steady herself as she followed. The corridor was longer than a bowling alley, and the carpet runner was worn thin as lint.

"The noise is getting louder," Luna whispered.

"The scent is getting strawberry-er," assured Claire.

At the curved staircase's landing lurked a moonfaced grandfather clock. In the shadows, it looked like a skinny giant.

"This place needs night-lights," Luna whispered.

As if in answer, an electric zing of lightning lit up the hall, and for an instant revealed a slim, dark-haired boy who was standing still as ice next to the clock.

"Shadows and shape-shifters!" Claire gasped. "It's the boy from the tapestry!"

Thunder boomed in answer.

"I saw him, too," squeaked Luna. Every hair on her head stood up in fright. She clapped a hand over her mouth to stifle a scream.

"Who goes there?" hissed Claire. She inched

toward the apparition. "Are you the fierce, ghostly ogre of Glenn Bly?"

"I am a ghost, yes. But I am hardly an ogre, and my proper name is Sir Percival Quilty," the boy whispered back. "Who art thou?"

"I'm Luna Bundkin, and that's my sister, Claire," piped up Luna. The longer Luna looked, the less spooky the ghost seemed. Except for his medieval clothes and his wan complexion, Sir Percival might have been any old eighth grader from Tower Hill Middle School.

"Ta, you strawberry-scented specter! We found you!" exclaimed Claire. "Our very first night in Scotland, and we nabbed the ghost of Glenn Bly!"

"Speaking freely, I believe the fact of the matter is that I have nabbed you," retorted Sir Percival. "This is my castle! 'Tis a mystery how you both can see my phantom image, but by the troth of my knighthood, I order you to depart from Glenn Bly at once!" He shook his phantom finger at them.

"Why?" asked Claire. "We just got here!"

"Plus, we haven't done anything wrong," said Luna.

"Ye must depart, nitwits, because the castle is guarded and protected by me," said Percival, his voice cracking. "Haven't ye heard my warning?" He lifted the silver amulet that hung around his neck and shook it.

Jingle-jingle. Clinkity-clink.

Luna scoffed. "But that's hardly a haunt at all! I could haunt this castle with my eyes closed and one hand tied behind my back!"

To prove it, she shut her eyes, stuck a hand behind her back, and cast the one ghost-ish spell she knew, the Chain Chant. It went like this:

> *My ghostie haunts the attic; my ghoulie haunts the eaves.*
> *They'll drag their chains and spread their gloom,*
> *They'll chase my friends from room to room.*
> *'Til everybody leaves!*

As soon as Luna finished, a terrible clanking and scraping sounded over their heads.

"Horrors! 'Tis the sound of iron chains dragged across the floor. Stop it at once!" Sir Percival hunched his shoulders to his ears.

Luna smirked. She was very good at the Chain Chant spell. The last time she had used it was at Frieda Gunderson's sleepover party, and everyone had been so scared that they had voted to keep the bathroom light on all night.

Claire was laughing. "You outspooked our ghost, Loon!"

Luna snapped her fingers to stop the spell. She didn't want to wake up anybody.

Boom!

Thunder! All three of them jumped. Sir Percival jumped highest.

"I guess you didn't conjure up this thunderstorm, did you?" asked Luna.

"Conjure a storm? Me? Why, I am not a spell-casting witch!" protested Sir Percival. A thoughtful expression crossed his face. "Ach, but ye maidens are, aren't ye? Ye see and hear me with special, witch-y senses."

"That's right. Claire and I are one-point-five-star witches. Good detectiving, Sir Percival," said Luna. She wanted to give the knight a compliment, since his haunting had been so pitiful.

"Percival, why do you smell like a strawberry patch?" asked Claire.

"'Tis a long tale," replied Sir Percival. "To begin at the beginning, which would be some time in the eleventh century, good folk used to grow—"

But just then, a tiny object whistled past Luna's ear and landed on the carpet.

"What is that?" cried the frightened young knight. He leaned down to look. "How odd. A moonlike sphere, no larger than a wee sparrow's skull."

"It's a golf ball," said Luna.

Now footsteps pattered down the corridor.

"Who goes there?" hissed Claire.

"Fred Bramblewine, your grandfather, goes here!" Grampy, dressed in his pajamas, came tiptoeing down the hall. He was holding a golf club.

"I thought I had this area to myself." Grampy blinked. "Anyone seen my golf ball?" He looked right past Percival.

"The doddering old-timer does not possess the witch-sense to observe me," said Percival.

"Don't call Grampy a doddering old-timer. He's very good at golf," whispered Luna.

"Aha!" said Grampy, picking up the ball, which was right next to Percival's toe. "Found ya!"

"Grampy!" Claire exclaimed. "Why are you up so late?"

"I'm practicing my putt," Grampy explained sheepishly. "Tomorrow is the first round of the golf tournament. I want to impress your grandmother." He put a finger to his lips. "But I don't think she needs to know about any of our late-night shenanigans. I won't tell if you won't. Let's go, girls. Back to bed."

Then Grampy placed one hand on each twin's shoulder, and steered Luna and Claire down the hallway.

When Luna turned around to check on their ghost, Sir Percival Quilty had disappeared.

"But he'll be back," Luna predicted after Grampy had dropped them off at Elderberry Chamber.

Claire yawned. "Listen, the rain is only a sprinkle now."

The twins jumped into their soft ocean of a feather bed and smoothed the covers evenly so they wouldn't fight over them later. "I can't wait to tell Grandy that we found Percy, the not-very-spooky, strawberry-smelling ghost." Claire sighed. "That was an easy mystery to solve."

"Nothing's solved yet, Clairsie," said Luna. "I don't mean to be a doomsday prophet, but my witch-hunch says it doesn't add up." She plumped her pillow and smoothed the ruffles of her nightgown. "We found a friendly ghost, not a fierce one. Crumbs, Sir Percival can hardly haunt. But what if there are some other, real baddies around this castle? And what if Grandy wants us to pop them?" Luna shivered. "Aren't you a teensy little bit scared, Clairsie? Clairsie?"

From the other side of the bed came the sound of a snore.

Obviously, Claire was not too scared. Luna's twin had fallen fast asleep.

4

Bloatus

THE NEXT MORNING, Claire woke to sunshine filtering though the windows of Elderberry Chamber. Good, no more rain. But then she saw an empty pocket of space under the quilt where Luna had been.

"Haggis and hailstones, I must've overslept!"

She decided to skip showering. When she raced downstairs to the kitchen, she found that everyone had already enjoyed breakfast. Mac, Luna, and Daphne were now doing after-breakfast chores. Mac was sweeping the floor, Luna was stacking the dishes, and Daphne was polishing the silverware.

A bed-and-breakfast castle was a lot of work, thought Claire. She was glad her own home back in Philadelphia did not double as a hotel.

"Hullo, Claire!" greeted Mac when he saw her. "Your grandparents told me to tell you that they'll be playing golf all day. However, Daphne and Luna will wait for you. Get a bite to eat, and after we finish up the morning chores, Daphne said she'd show you the grounds."

"Okay," said Claire. Crumbs! she thought. If Grandy was off at golf, that meant she and Luna would have to wait all day before they could tell her about Sir Percival.

Meanwhile, it looked as if there was no escaping morning chores, or spending the day with Miss Daphne Bly.

Claire took a long time eating her bowl of something called muesli, cereal that tasted sort of like Oatie-oats, but better. Then she got to work helping Mac, angling the dustpan in those hard-to-sweep places.

"Thanks, Claire," said Mac when they were done. "I'm stepping out to tend the stables now, so come 'round later if you want to exercise the horses. Think that might be fun?"

"Aye!" Claire had never been horseback riding, but she hoped she could make her horse go faster than Daphne's.

"As long as my horse doesn't go too fast," said Luna.

That's when Claire noticed that her twin looked terrified.

And Miss Daphne Bly was looking very mischievous, indeed.

What was that pesky lass up to?

Once Mac left, Claire found out.

"Oh, Claire! All morning, Daphne has been telling me such terrible things about the history of Glenn Bly!" Luna wailed. "So many wars and tortures. Tell her, Daphne. Tell Claire some of your stories."

"Just the usual rot," said Daphne as she eyed Claire. "Battles, bloodshed, and beheadings."

Claire shrugged. She did not scare as easily as her twin. "All castles have gory ancient histories."

"True enough, American Claire," Daphne admitted, "but I've saved the worst for last."

"Daphne says Glenn Bly is haunted by a fierce and evil ogre," Luna gasped. "I knew it! I knew there was a *real* baddie lurking."

"Yeah, yeah. I heard about the ogre yesterday. But what I want to know is, where is he now?" Claire asked.

"Oh, everywhere and anywhere," Daphne answered.

"Ever seen him?"

"Yes, but not recently."

"What's he look like?"

"Hunchback, slimy, bit of a purplish gash on his eyeball."

"What does he eat?"

"Wild mushrooms and little dogs."

"What's his name?"

"Bloatus."

"How'd you know his name?" Claire asked.

"Did he tell you? Have you spoken to him?"

At so many questions, Daphne clammed up.

"Or maybe . . . your Bloatus is bogus," Claire accused.

"I'm not a liar!" Daphne retorted, her cheeks flaming pink. "Bloatus is real, and he's dreadful! He watches over my grandfather and me, but he despises everyone else. I'm quite surprised he hasn't tried to scare you by now!" She quirked an eyebrow. "Are you sure you didn't hear Bloatus last night, jangling and clinking his bloody spiked chain?"

Claire exchanged a look with her twin. Yes, they had heard a jangling, all right. But it had turned out to be the not-at-all spooky jingle-jangling of puny Percival Quilty.

"I've got an idea. Let's go horseback riding and see if we can find Bloatus anywhere. Then Luna and I'll decide if we're scared of him or not," challenged Claire.

Daphne looked startled. Then firm. "Very well. I'll go put on my riding clothes," she said, and she flounced out of the kitchen.

Once the twins were alone, Claire noticed that over her jeans, Luna was wearing a long, white, lacy something-or-other.

"Loon! What nutty outfit have you got on now?"

"Don't tell Mom," answered Luna, "but it's her special holiday tablecloth. I thought it would be pretty as a skirt. Sort of romantic and olden days-ish."

Claire shook her head at her sister. "I won't tell, if you lend me some of your clothes. I forgot to pack some stuff."

"I knew it!" Now it was Luna's turn to shake her head at her sister.

After a quick shower and a change back into her same clothes from yesterday (with fresh socks and underwear that she borrowed from Luna) Claire was ready for riding.

Mac and Daphne were already at the stables waiting for them. Daphne was dressed in full riding gear, in special riding pants and long boots.

Show-off, thought Claire.

Mac had saddled up the horses.

"Daphne has the most riding experience, so she'll take T.J.," Mac decided. "Claire, I think you ought to try Dooley. He's frisky, but he responds well to your command. And for you Luna, here is Paloma. She's gentle as a dove."

Claire hoisted herself up onto chestnut-brown, sturdy Dooley. Her witch-smarts clicked instantly with the horse. (Most witches have a pretty good understanding of animal moods.)

T.J. was a black pony with white markings and a hot temper, but Daphne swung up as if she had been riding him for years.

Claire glanced over at Luna. She seemed glad to be on sleepy Paloma, a mare that did not look as if she would be moving faster than a tricycle.

Daphne high-stepped T.J. in a circle, showing off. She was the only Scottish lass Claire had ever met, but she certainly was irritating.

But Claire knew how to irritate, too.

"We're off to see the ogre," Claire sang under her breath, just loud enough for Daphne to hear. "The wonderful ogre of Bly."

"Don't go too far or fast." Mac gave his

granddaughter a meaningful look. "Daphne, I'm trusting you to keep pace with Paloma."

"Shall do!" Daphne clicked the reins. She signaled for the twins to follow her.

In the morning cold, the fog was as thick as chowder, but the fields were open and flat, perfect for a leisurely ride.

"Let's head for the hills," Claire suggested.

"Let's go around the orchard," suggested Daphne.

They both looked at Luna to be the tiebreaker.

"Orchard," said Luna.

Daphne smirked.

Claire scowled. Her twin's politeness always got in the way of fun.

"Before the Battle of Sodden Field destroyed them, wild strawberry patches grew all along these meadows," explained Daphne with a sweep of her hand. "Glenn Bly was famous for its strawberries. People served them in everything. Strawberry salad, strawberry mashed potatoes, strawberry sauce on strawberry shepherd's pie. In fact, the Bly coat of arms is a giant strawberry."

"Your family has its own coat of arms?" asked Luna.

"Of course," said Daphne airily. "Doesn't everybody?"

Claire gritted her teeth.

They trotted through the orchard and over a low bridge that crossed a brook. "I'm fairly sure that this is where Bloatus lives," said Daphne as she stopped T.J. on the bridge and peered down into the water's dark depths. "He might not show himself this morning, but you soon will feel his presence. I just hope you don't feel his awful, angry wrath! Let me try to summon him."

Her face pinched in concentration.

Soon came the faint sound of *jingle-clink.*

"Aha! Hear that? That is Bloatus's war call!" said Daphne. She frowned as she looked at the twins. "Aren't you even a wee bit scared?"

"That depends on who's scaring us." Claire sniffed the telltale scent of strawberries. She had a hunch that whoever was on the other end of the *jingle-clink* was not too scary. "Come out, come out, wherever you are!" she sang.

From behind a cypress tree, Sir Percival Quilty appeared on his silver steed. Although he seemed less scrawny now that he was saddled on his ghostly horse, Percival did not fit the description of an awful ogre. As he approached the bridge, Claire saw that he held his amulet between his fingers, and was jingling it so hard that his tongue was sticking out from the effort.

Daphne was still looking down at the water. She could hear the jingle-clink, but she could not see Sir Percival. "Yes," she said, pointing down, "the noise is coming from under the bridge."

Claire popped open her eyes and pretended to chatter her teeth, making a fake scared expression for Luna, who laughed. Percival saw Claire's phony frightened face, too.

"Do not insult me, ye doubting twins," snapped Percival. "'Tis plenty scarier if ye cannot see me or hear my voice! Then ye have to use your imagination, like the damsel Daphne."

From the look on her face, Daphne seemed

to be using a huge amount of imagination. And Claire could bet that Daphne had imagined something far worse than Sir Percival.

When Percival reached up and snapped a few twigs off the tree, Daphne gasped.

"Did you hear the crackle of breaking bones?" Her eyes rounded. "It's said that the ogre Bloatus slaughtered fifty men in a single day. Aren't you scared?"

"Oh, yes, I'm scared," said Luna politely.

"You are?" asked Daphne.

"No, ye are not! And I have had enough of you, you impertinent, identical witch twins!" grumbled Percival. "I am off. Heigh-ho, Duncan!" With that, Percival tapped his horse's flanks and, turning from the bridge, lightly spurred him off.

"Wait!" Claire picked up her reins and clicked Dooley into a gallop. She clattered over the bridge in quick pursuit of the ghost.

"Claire!" yelled Daphne. "Where are you going?" She started to give chase.

"Daphne, *n-o-o-o!* Mac said you had to stay with me and Paloma!" cried Luna. "I don't want to be all alone on the bridge at the mercy of this wild horse."

"Oh, brother!" exclaimed Daphne. "Paloma is about as wild as a bowl of soup." But she turned her horse to stay with Luna.

Good, thought Claire. She needed to speak to the ghost knight in private. "Wait up, Percival!" she cried as she caught up to his side.

"Go away, thou witch," said Percival.

"I'm sorry," said Claire. "I didn't mean to laugh at your haunting."

"Contrary to what thou mightest think," said Percival stiffly, "I have been rather good at haunting the castle till now. I even got a nice mention in the *Spookiest Scottish Castles Tour Guide Book*." He shrugged. "Alas, witches must be harder to scare. Of which clan art thou?"

"Bramblewine."

The knight crooked his eyebrow. "Art thou up to mischief? The Bramblewine witches are famous for their four-star pranks."

"I'm not up to four stars yet," Claire

admitted. Then she quickly changed the subject. "Percival, why are you haunting Glenn Bly?" she asked. "I mean, a ghost can't be good for a bed-and-breakfast. There's even a sign posted out front that says 'Glenn Bly Welcomes You.' How can guests feel welcome if they're also being haunted?"

Sir Percival seemed to think about that. "My knightly duty is to protect Glenn Bly as best I can," he said. "The castle is in danger. That is all I know. Now I must be off. Next time, witch girl, thou ought to act more scared, even if it is only pretend. 'Tis rude to laugh at a ghost."

With that, he vanished into the mist.

Claire watched him with envy. In her Little Book of Shadows, Vanishing into Mist was a four-star-level spell.

She trotted back to the others.

"American Claire, do you always run off to have conversations with yourself?" asked Daphne as they wound the horses back toward the castle.

"Not always. But sometimes," Claire answered honestly.

"Well, it's very rude," said Daphne.

Claire did not answer. She was getting used to people telling her she was rude.

As they came closer to the castle, Daphne slowed T.J. to a stop. The reins went slack in her hands.

"Oh, no," she breathed.

"Oh, no, who?" asked Luna.

"Oh, no, where?" asked Claire.

"Oh, no, *that*." Daphne pointed. "That big, silver car in the middle of the front lawn. The notorious Rolls-Royce."

Now both twins caught sight of the large luxury car parked smack in the middle of the castle's front lawn.

"Whose notorious silver Rolls-Royce?" asked Claire.

Claire saw that Daphne's face had become rather pale. "The notorious silver Rolls-Royce of Lord and Lady Shrillingbird," said Daphne. "The dreadful owners of Glenn Bly."

5
The Shrillingbirds

ACCORDING TO DAPHNE, Lord and Lady Shrillingbird were the pickiest, grouchiest, complaining-est couple in all of Scotland. Flowers sagged and soufflés flopped in their presence. Cats growled. Dogs hid. Nothing was ever good enough for the Shrillingbirds. They hated everything.

Especially things that matched or came in pairs.

"That's why I expect they'll hate twins most

of all. So when they're mean to you, don't pay them any mind," Daphne warned after she, Luna, and Claire had unsaddled, watered, and brushed down the horses before heading from the stables toward the castle.

"Okay, but why are they here in the first place?" asked Luna. She was already nervous about meeting the Shrillingbirds. Her tablecloth skirt had become a little bit muddy during the riding, and her face was slightly sweaty.

"Because they know my grandfather will serve them a free lunch," Daphne explained. "Even though they've got heaps of pounds, they're too cheap to go to a restaurant."

Luna nodded knowledgeably. She knew that a Scottish *pound* meant money. It was similar to an American dollar. What Daphne meant by *heaps of pounds* was not that the Shrillingbirds were super-fatties, but super-rich.

"Chin up," said Daphne as they marched through the castle doors.

But poor Daphne seemed less like her normal self, Luna thought. From the moment she'd caught sight of the silver Rolls-Royce, her sly good humor had disappeared. Now her chin was up and her eyes looked bright and blinky, as if she might even cry.

The Shrillingbirds were seated in the grand dining hall, at a table that could have served twenty people on one side and twenty people on the other. Lord Shrillingbird sat at the foot, carefully eating a steak with a fork and knife. Lady Shrillingbird sat at the head, sloppily drinking broth from a bowl. Some of the broth was running down her chin.

Mac was serving them lunch. His face was rosy from so many trips up and down, up and down, from one end of the table and back again. The Shrillingbirds did not seem to notice.

"More lemonade," shrilled Lady Shrillingbird.

"Pass the salt," shrilled Lord Shrillingbird.

"Right-o," wheezed Mac. "Hullo, girls. Daphne, would you be a love and help me serve the toffee cake for Lady S, and the plum pudding for Lord S?"

"Certainly, Grandpop," said Daphne, and she followed Mac into the kitchen, leaving the twins alone with the Shrillingbirds.

Luna looked the Shrillingbirds up and down, then down and up.

Lady Shrillingbird was very, very red and square as a small brick.

Lord Shrillingbird was very, very gray and round as a large stone.

Both of them had been preoccupied with their lunches, but as soon as both Shrillingbirds caught sight of Luna and Claire, they let out identical screams.

"Ew! Disgusting! Twins!" they cried in unison. Then they glared across the table at each other.

"My lord, don't copy what I say," said Lady Shrillingbird.

"In this instance, my lady, you copied what I said," said Lord Shrillingbird.

Lady Shrillingbird sniffed. "We hate anything that comes in pairs or matched sets," she told Luna. "Especially matching bedside table lamps, or matched socks, or matched earrings. Get it? No match." She shook her head, so that Luna could see she wore a diamond stud earring in one ear, and a swinging plastic yellow daisy earring in the other ear.

"Get it? No match." Lord Shrillingbird flutter-kicked his feet out from under the table. He was wearing one red polka-dotted sock, and one flowered sock with a ruffle.

"We also hate rhymes," continued Lady Shrillingbird. "Because a rhyme is a word match. But matching *people* are worst of all. Do your names rhyme, you repulsive twins?"

"I'm Luna," said Luna.

"And I'm Tuna," said Claire.

The Shrillingbirds gaped in horror. Luna cut a look at her sister, who wrinkled her nose witchishly.

Daphne and Mac swung out of the kitchen. Daphne shoved a plate of toffee cake in front of Lady Shrillingbird, while Mac served Lord Shrillingbird his plum pudding.

"Overall, my lunch was too tough and bitter,"

announced Lady Shrillingbird.

"Specifically, my steak was mushy, had too many hot spices, and left an aftertaste that coated my tongue as if I'd been licking mold," said Lord Shrillingbird.

"I'm sorry about your lunches," stammered Mac.

"Luckily, we're staying through the weekend," said Lady Shrillingbird. "So we shall allow you to prepare more meals. Perhaps you'll have better luck next time."

"Through the weekend?" repeated Daphne faintly.

Lord and Lady Shrillingbird ignored her. Lady Shrillingbird turned to her husband. "Now then, my lord, let's walk around our castle. I've got some divine decorating suggestions for when we move in. And after our walk, we'll have a nap in the Peacock Chamber."

"Isn't that our grandparents' room?" asked Claire.

Lord and Lady Shrillingbird ignored her.

"Be it ever so humble, there's no place like

our second home!" sang Lord Shrillingbird.

The Shrillingbirds gulped their desserts in a couple of bites, then pranced out of the dining room arm in arm, leaving a messy trail of crumbs behind.

"Are the Shrillingbirds planning to move into your castle?" exclaimed Luna.

Mac nodded sadly. "I'm afraid so. I had to sell Glenn Bly to the Shrillingbirds a few years ago because I couldn't afford the steep castle taxes. Now we run the bed-and-breakfast business and pay them rent. For a while, the situation worked fine. That is, until the Shrillingbirds decided to sell their bungalow in Baja, their salon in Singapore, and their manor in Monte Carlo. Recently, they've decided this place would make a nice holiday castle."

Mac glanced sidelong at his granddaughter. "I never imagined the Shrillingbirds would want to live in a crumbling castle. But they are such unpleasant company, I'm afraid that they would be terribly difficult to share this space with. Daphne and I would most likely have to move."

Daphne, her chin up, did not answer. Instead, she stacked the Shrillingbirds' dirty plates and cups and swept out of the dining room without a word. Then came the sound of a giant clattering and bashing as Daphne dumped the dishes in the sink.

"Poor lass," said Mac. "She has lived through her ups and downs, but Glenn Bly is the only home she's ever known. Now, girls, leave the cleanup to us. I need to go cheer my grand-daughter."

"Sure, Mac," said the twins.

Quietly, they stole upstairs to Elderberry Chamber.

"I feel sorry for Daphne," said Luna. "We've lived through our ups and downs, too. But we've only lived them in one place, good old Twenty-two Locust Street. And no awful people are looking to crowd us out."

"It not a crumbling castle with a goofy ghost," said Claire, "but I love-love-love our home."

"Even if you can hear Justin practice Hacky

Sack through the wall," Luna mentioned.

"And even if we have to share a room," Claire added.

"And even if the radiator pipes squeak in the winter."

"And even if our kittens shredded up the new red-and-green-flowered living room curtains."

"They did?" Luna cringed.

Claire nodded. "Better not tell Mom. Hey, that reminds me. Let's see what's happening at home. Did you bring your spy globe? I forgot mine."

"I've got mine right here." Luna ran to her suitcase and pulled out her spy globe. It was the size and weight of a glass baseball, and not at all magical looking.

But when Luna shook it, every color appeared and swirled inside it like a liquid rainbow. She fogged the globe with her breath and set it on the windowsill.

"Show us our family," commanded Luna.

The twins peered into the globe. Soon the

fog and colors faded to produce the globe's first image.

"Hey, it's Justin. He's sitting on a bench," said Luna. "He looks so bored. That's funny. I thought he was playing football all week."

"He's in his uniform, though," noted Claire. "Maybe he only goes on the field during emergencies. When the team needs someone who can really clobber."

Next, Claire breathed on the glass to change the image.

"Aw. It's Mom and Steve eating breakfast and reading the morning paper," said Luna.

"And Steve is sneak-feeding turkey-bacon scraps to Edie and Hortense," added Claire. "I'm happy he remembered that kittens need treats."

"But why are they eating breakfast when we just had lunch?" Luna tapped the globe. "Strange. Is this thing screening reruns?"

"No, dummy. It's five hours later here. Scotland afternoon time is Pennsylvania breakfast time."

"Oh, yeah." Embarrassed, Luna breathed on

the glass to change the image once again.

"Aw. It's Fluffy and Dad strolling Bert through the park," said Claire.

"And Bert is still bald and he still looks like a toad," Luna observed. "I hope he fills out soon."

Together, the twins breathed on the glass.

"Bagpipes and beefsteak, there's Grandy!" Claire exclaimed.

"She looks really peeved!" Luna drew back.

"Because I am peeved!" thundered a voice behind them.

"Grandy!" The twins turned to see their grandmother standing in the doorway.

"What are you doing back already?" asked Luna.

"Your grandfather and I lost today's round early. Dead last," growled Grandy.

"Sorry, Grandy," said Claire. "Is that why you're in a bad mood?"

"No. The reason I'm in a bad mood is because I was looking forward to coming home for a nap in *my* room, and what do I find but two ghastly people sleeping in *my* bed!" Grandy scowled. "When your grandfather and I woke them up and tried to shove them off, they threw their pillows at us!"

"Sounds like the Shrillingbirds," said Claire.

"Grandy, those are the owners of Glenn Bly," said Luna. "Technically, it's *their* bed." She tried to say this nicely, so that her grandmother would not get grumpier.

"By the way, we found the ghost," said Claire. "His name's Sir Percival. If you want to cast a spell to make him leave, I don't think it will matter much. He's not very spooky."

"Oh, good work, twins," said Grandy, her face brightening. "That's the best news I've heard all day! Go get him so I can pop him! And while I'm at it, I might as well get rid of those Squawkingbirds. Your poor grandfather had to go walk in the garden to calm his nerves. Nobody's ever thrown a pillow at Fred before. It was quite a shock to his system."

Luna opened her mouth to suggest that perhaps her grandmother should proceed with caution. Now that she'd met Percival, it seemed mean to pop him. Also, getting rid of the Shrillingbirds seemed like it would be hard work. In general, Luna did not think it was a very safe or smart plan to make people vanish just because you could. But she wasn't sure how to say all this to Grandy.

"Don't stand there with you mouth hanging open." Grandy snapped her fingers. "Bring me the ghost for popping! Meet me in the Peacock Chamber in two minutes. Get moving!"

Luna shut her mouth again.

After all, Grandy was a five-star witch. She knew best. Right?

6
Popped and Foiled

CLAIRE AND LUNA found Sir Percival in his regular haunt, hiding behind the clock on the hallway landing. When he caught sight of the twins, he leaped out at them.

"Boo! Did I scare you?" he asked.

"Not really," said Claire. She turned and whispered behind her hand to Luna. "How could Daphne think that you-know-who is s-c-a-r-y?"

"Excuse me, thou rude witch, but I know

how to spell!" exclaimed Sir Percival.

"Sorry, Sir P," said Claire. "Anyway, we have a proposition for you. Since you say you're so good at castle haunting, Luna and I thought it might be fun-fun-fun for you to give our grandmother a little spook." Claire smiled her most warm and coaxing smile. "She's a teeny old lady. I bet she'd jump right out of her boots if she saw a genuine ghost!"

"Thinks thou so?" Sir Percival looked doubtful.

"Oh, yes," said Claire, taking his hand, which slipped out of her grasp because it was a ghost hand, and not made out of skin and bones, but ghost dew.

"Well . . . it would be good fun to scare a teeny old lady," said Percival with a gleam in his eye. "Let us be off, then, and be quick."

Seeing the swagger in his ghostly step and the confident ghost-grin on Percival's face as they marched toward the Peacock Chamber, Claire felt almost sorry for the puny phantom.

Luna must have felt the same way.

"Crumbs! Percival's not a gruesome ghost, Clairsie," whispered Luna (in a secret witch-whisper so that Percival could not hear). "I'd even say he's a sweet addition to Glenn Bly. Having Percival in the castle is like having a mouse in your house, or a garden gnome."

"I'm with you, Loon. But the reason we're here is to help get rid of a ghost," reminded Claire. "That's what Grandy wants, and that's what we'll deliver."

Luna sneaked another look at the knight. "Poor Percival. He doesn't stand a chance against Grandy, does he?"

"Nope," Claire agreed, but rules were rules. She and Luna needed to help the Blys. Besides, Claire had a secret hope. What if helping to pop a ghost meant getting an extra half star? Another half a star would make her and Luna full two-star witches! Although the Decree Keepers were often stingy with their star rewards, ghost-popping seemed like a good, smart, and tricky spell.

Claire could almost see those two bright stars shining on her dark velvet witch robe. She crossed her fingers and kissed them for luck.

When the twins plus Percival entered the Peacock Chamber, Grandy was waiting. Hands on her hips, she stood at the foot of the mahogany bed with a horrible scowl on her face.

"What a nasty sight," she muttered.

In the bed, Lord and Lady Shrillingbird were fast asleep. They looked extremely comfortable snoozing under the greeny-blue, peacock-patterned quilt. Lady Shrillingbird was wearing plaid flannel pajamas and Lord Shrillingbird was wearing silky white pajamas trimmed with pink satin roses.

But both the Shrillingbirds slept identically, with their noses pointing up at the ceiling and their mouths open, and traces of lunch on their chins.

"Your grandmother is a bit taller than teeny," mentioned Percival as he clinked his amulet in his usual hopeful haunting manner.

"Aha!" cried Grandy, with a fierce look that struck Percival into silence. "I've got ya now!" And before the knight could think up a good ghostly defense, Grandy wheeled on Percival, hopped on one foot, wriggled her fingers, and with full, five-star vengeance, cast:

> "*Ancient castle, scrawny ghost,*
> *Go and haunt who needs thee most!*
> *Take thee to a—*"

But before she could get any further, *pop!* With a dry, sparkling scatter of dust, Percival was gone.

On the floor where he'd been now rested a luscious, red strawberry.

Poor Percival! thought Claire.

"Oh, poor Percival." Luna echoed Claire's thoughts out loud. "Where did he go?"

"Who knows and who cares? Maybe he's off haunting a smaller bed-and-breakfast," said Grandy. "This castle was much too big a job for one measly ghost." She squinted at the strawberry. "Blech. Ghost dropping."

The twins watched as Grandy reached for her pocketbook on the dresser, pulled out a tissue, then stooped to pick up the strawberry, which she threw in the wastepaper basket.

"I guess that's that," Grandy cackled, wiping her hands. "Heh-heh-heh. What a cinch. He was weaker than I thought. Did you notice how I didn't even need the whole spell? Well, live and learn. Now for the hard part."

She rolled up the sleeves of her windbreaker and turned her attention to the slumbering Shrillingbirds.

Claire was glad Grandy was getting rid of the Shrillingbirds. They were loud and piggy and obnoxious—twenty times worse than poor Percival.

The twins looked on respectfully as Grandy hopped on her other foot and cast:

"Baked cod, whipped cream, and wet
   wool socks
Can all turn bad and rotten.
So do pillow-throwing guests—
Be gone, and be forgotten!"

Zip! Zam! Zim! Electric blue-white light charged around the bed. The twins stepped back in awe.

Lord Shrillingbird wheezed. Lady Shrillingbird sneezed. Both of them twitched slightly. But neither of them disappeared.

"Hmm. They're stickier than I thought," said Grandy. "All right-y. I can play that game, you icky stickers." She thought a moment, wiped her brow, hopped in a furious circle, and recast her spell:

> *"I'll make a dragon burn you up,*
> *Or feed you to a goat!*
> *Let's drop you from the highest ledge*
> *Into a slimy moat!"*

She snapped, wriggled, and did a little rumba. (The rumba was not part of the spell. Grandy had been taking lessons.)

With this fearsome five-star spell, the entire bed trembled, lifted an inch off the floor, and hung suspended in midair. Then it dropped with a mighty, thudding crash.

The Shrillingbirds, however, stayed put.

In fact, they did not even wake up. Lord Shrillingbird made a gurgling sleep-sound. A thin spool of drool oozed from Lady Shrillingbird's mouth down her cheek.

And now, in the corner of the room came a *baaaaaa*.

Claire, Luna, and Grandy turned. In the corner of the room, a little black goat was standing, contentedly chewing on a piece of the peacock-patterned carpet.

"Curses! Foiled again!" Grandy looked mad enough to spit.

"What's with the goat?" asked Claire.

"Eh, foiled-spell side effect," said Grandy.

"What is going on, Grandy?" asked Luna. "Why aren't the Shrillingbirds responding to your spells?"

Grandy looked embarrassed. "It almost never, ever happens, but there are a few people in the world who are completely resistant to five-star spells," she said. "Their horrible personalities protect them like a shield." She shook her head, bewildered. "I haven't seen such wretched resistance since that time I tried to send Madame DuFarge, my seventh-grade French teacher, back to Paris."

She gestured weakly at the Shrillingbirds. "I could cast five-star spells on this pair of twits all day, but I'll never be able to budge them."

Claire felt a pull of something like sadness in her heart. *Crumbs.* She had always thought that her grandmother could do anything.

They all looked down at the Shrillingbirds, who continued to snooze, not knowing that their special, awful-personality powers had warded off a famous five-star witch's most magnificent spells.

Even the goat crept up to get a look at the spell-defying duo. Then his attention turned to Lord Shrillingbird's fluffy rabbit-hair bedroom slipper. He picked it up and took a curious nibble.

"I think the Shrillingbirds are staying at Glenn Bly through the weekend," said Luna.

"Drat." Grandy wrinkled her nose. "I'm not surprised, though. Bad houseguests always outstay their welcome. Well, maybe I can cast a one-star spell to move them. Nobody can escape a one-star spell. They're small, but they itch. Like mosquito bites. All right—here goes."

With one finger, Grandy traced a circle in the air, pointed at the Shrillingbirds, and in a discouraged voice, cast the new spell:

"Since you two will not disappear—
At least don't let me find you here."

The bed was swallowed up by a puff of smoke that smelled like scrambled eggs. When the smoke cleared, the Shrillingbirds were gone, and the peacock-patterned quilt was hospital smooth, with one corner turned down invitingly.

"Wow, good one, Grandy," said Luna.

"Not really," said Grandy grumpily. "I didn't move them far."

"Where did you move them?" asked Claire.

"Into your bed, of course," said Grandy. "Okay, time for my nap. Well, at least I got rid of that blasted ghost." Grandy knocked off her shoes and crawled into bed, fluffing the pillow. "If you run into your grandfather, send him back to me. As you know, he gets very cranky if he doesn't have his afternoon nap. Now. Girls— goat—begone!"

With that, Grandy sniffed in one nostril, then the other.

In the *poof!* of the next moment, both twins, one goat, and Lord Shrillingbird's fluffy slipper all got scooped up, swept off, and dropped outside Glenn Bly's back door, where Grandy had instaported them.

Ancient Room, Secret Book

"THERE YOU ARE!" cried Daphne, running out the kitchen door toward Luna and Claire. "I've been looking all over for you two." She stopped and stared. "Heavens to Pete! Whose goat is that?"

But the goat had seen enough strange things at the Castle Glenn Bly for one day, and he did not want to stick around to see any more. He threw back his head and released a raspy bleat.

Then he picked up Lord Shrillingbird's slipper, kicked up his hind legs, and bounded off toward the fields where he'd been wandering, looking for thistles, before Grandy's spell had nabbed him.

Suddenly, low clouds swept over the sky.

"Oh, no! Not another thunderstorm!" cried Daphne, looking up. "How peculiar! We never get this much rain, usually. And it comes on so fast! Run inside, and hurry, before you get soaked!"

Shrieking, the threesome dashed into the kitchen just as sheets of rain began to wash down heavily over the land.

"Here's an idea," said Daphne, shaking the rain from her hair. "We explored the outside of Glenn Bly this morning, so why don't I take you exploring the inside of the castle this afternoon?"

"Oh, good!" Luna clapped her hands together. She liked doing indoorsy things a lot better than outdoorsy things, and she hadn't much enjoyed the morning's horseback ride. Even a slowpoke horse such as Paloma had made her nervous. But exploring the castle would give her a chance to pretend she was a princess. Pretending to be a princess was one of Luna's favorite games.

"I'll be the tour guide," Daphne announced. "We'll begin with the cellar and climb our way up to the bell tower. The stairs are just off the butler's pantry. This way!"

Luna could tell that Claire did not care for Daphne's bossiness. But Luna didn't mind it. Actually, Daphne and Claire were a lot alike— and Luna didn't mind Claire's bossiness, either.

Mostly, Luna was just happy to tour the castle. She had never seen another castle other than Glenn Bly, but she bet this was the best one in Scotland. A castle would be the perfect setting for a splendid summer wedding. (Luna loved-loved-loved weddings, especially the splendid summer kind.)

"Even if we spent all afternoon, we still wouldn't be able to see every room at Glenn Bly," Daphne said as they wound down the steps to the cellar. "It takes nine hours to walk the castle from top to bottom. I timed myself."

"Let's try to beat your time!" said Claire. "Let's try to explore the whole castle in four and a half hours."

"Let's not and say we did," said Daphne.

"Let's!" insisted Claire.

They both stopped and looked at Luna to be tiebreaker.

"Let's not," said Luna. She hated to rush things.

Daphne smirked. Clare scowled. Then Daphne took Luna's hand. "Watch your step. It's dark down here."

The cellar was dark. It smelled like old pennies and was stacked from its cold, earthen floor to its beamed ceiling with heavy barrels that Daphne told them were ancient wine casks.

But wine casks aren't that interesting, even ancient ones, so the girls didn't stay down in the moldy cellar for long.

The airy, second-floor garden parlor was more like it. So was the yellow-silk-wallpapered music room, the fern-filled conservatory, and the gloomy portrait hall filled with gilt-framed faces of Blys gone by.

"Oh, Daphne, you're so lucky to live here!" said Luna.

"I suppose I am," said Daphne. "But I'm used to it. I've never lived anywhere else."

Behind her, Luna heard Claire sniff.

Next, she showed the twins into a library that made Grandy's den look like a nook. Its walls were hung with framed maps and inlaid with ebony wood. Overstuffed leather armchairs sat in front of a flagstone hearth. Most astounding of all, though, were its bookshelves.

"There are almost four thousand books in this room," Daphne told the twins. "I haven't read them all, of course. But I might have read, oh, perhaps two hundred."

Beside her, Luna heard Claire snort.

A narrow door stood beside one of the bookshelves. On its surface was carved a single strawberry, the Bly coat of arms. Though Luna and Claire spied the door at the same time, it was Claire who bounded over and wrenched it open without asking permission.

"Hey, look, there are secret stairs behind here!" she exclaimed. She stuck her head in the doorway. "Yoo-hoo-ooo!" The echo bounced up the stairwell. She popped her head out again. "Where do they lead?"

"Up to the charter room," Daphne answered. She ran to the door and closed it, then stood in front of it with her arms crossed. "But that room's not meant for visitors, American Claire. What is stored in the charter room is much too secret and valuable to be on display."

"Oh, we promise we won't tell anyone," said Luna. A secret room! How romantic! "Please, Daphne, will you show us?"

Claire bit her lips to keep silent. By now, both twins knew that Daphne would do a special favor for Luna, but not for Claire.

Daphne hesitated. Then she smiled at Luna. "I suppose it wouldn't hurt, just this once."

The staircase was tiny, built during a time when most people were tiny, too. With Daphne in the lead, Luna and Claire followed her up the stairs that got darker, dustier, steeper, and spookier as they climbed.

At the top of the stairs was another narrow door, which Daphne opened using a long key that hung from a nail in the wall. Luna held her breath as she pushed inside, expecting to be stunned by beautiful furnishings and fixtures.

To her surprise, the circle-shaped room was almost empty. Its only light trickled through a domed window that cast a weak light onto its single piece of furniture—a carved wooden table.

Open on the table rested a thick, brittle, crumbly book.

Luna's shoulders sagged. For so much top secrecy, this room was not very exciting at all.

She could tell her twin felt the same way. "Hmmph. What's so valuable about some dumb table?" scoffed Claire.

"It's not the *table* that's valuable, American Claire. It's the *book*," explained Daphne. She walked over to it and smoothed her hand over a page. "This is Glenn Bly's Book of All Records. It is the history of everything and anything in, on, or around Glenn Bly. Of crops and weather and holidays, of fishing and hunting and hawking seasons, of battles and plagues and droughts. It shows where wells were sunk and ships were wrecked and treasure was buried and thieves were hung. It's also a record of the births, marriages, and deaths of everyone who ever lived in, or even visited this castle. That book contains over one thousand years' worth of facts."

"Crumbs, that's old-old-old! Can we write our names in it?" asked Claire. She picked up the long quill pen that rested next to the book and eyed the pot of ink. "Even if we don't live here, we visited Glenn Bly all the way from Philadelphia, U.S.A. That's more than eight hours in two planes. It should count for something, shouldn't it?"

"'Fraid not!" Daphne plucked the quill from Claire's hands. "Visitors haven't signed this particular book for three hundred years. There's another guest book downstairs in the front hall, with a regular ink pen, for guests who want to write about the splendid view, or complain about the plumbing. You are free to sign that stupid book. Nobody reads it, anyway."

Claire snatched the quill back. "But I want to sign *this* book. Hmm, maybe I'll ask the Shrillingbirds for permission. Since it *is* the Shrillingbirds' castle," she teased.

"Claire's just making a bad joke," Luna interrupted quickly, taking the quill from her trouble-making twin and replacing it.

"I know." Daphne's chin stayed up, but it trembled. "But let me warn you now, American Claire, for your own good. Writing in the Book of All Records might stir up the wrath of our ghost." Her eyes darted around the room. "He could be watching us this very minute!"

"Actually, we have good news for you about that ghost, Daphne," Luna assured. "You don't have to worry about him anymore. He's gone."

"Gone? Gone?" To Luna's surprise, instead of being joyful, Daphne looked positively devastated. "What do you mean, gone?" she squeaked.

"As in, *See ya*. As in, *Good-bye*. As in, *Vamoose*," Claire clarified. "Trust us. Our grandmother is kind of an expert at kicking out ghosts."

"But if *he's* gone," said Daphne slowly, "that means *they'll* stay."

"Who?" asked Luna.

"Why, the *Shrillingbirds*, of course. They want to live at Glenn Bly. Bloatus was our last hope." Daphne's face was creased with worry. "He's been with us forever, always clinking and carrying on. I've never minded it. A ghost is a bit like having a mouse in your house."

"Or a garden gnome," added Claire.

Daphne nodded. "When Grandpop and I learned that the Shrillingbirds wanted to move here, he promised he'd come up with a plan. A plan to stop Lord and Lady Shrillingbird from wanting to live here." Daphne sighed. "To tell you the truth, for some reason I thought that perhaps you and your grandparents were part of the plan. But now I see that you've done just the opposite. Because if Bloatus is truly *gone*, then Lord and Lady Shrillingbird will take over Glenn Bly, and Grandpop and I'll have to move into a horrid, smelly flat in the city."

"Cities aren't horrid and smelly," countered Clare, "unless it's garbage night in the middle of August."

But both twins knew they'd made a mistake.

Grandy shouldn't have popped the Ghost of Glenn Bly after all. Not if Sir Percival was Mac and Daphne's only chance of keeping their castle.

"Don't worry, Daphne," said Luna. "We can make things right again."

She wasn't sure how. But the hope in Daphne's eyes made Luna resolve to give it her best.

"Girls!" came a shout from far, far below. "Dinner!"

"Already? Oh, no. We haven't explored the bell tower," said Luna.

"Another day," Daphne promised, squeezing her hand.

Closing up the charter room, the threesome ran downstairs to find the Shrillingbirds once again seated at the head and foot of the dining room table. Lady Shrillingbird was dressed in a safari suit, and Lord Shrillingbird was wearing a Hawaiian muumuu.

"Yuck, it's Luna and Tuna," squealed Lady Shrillingbird.

"Yuck," agreed Lord Shrillingbird.

"If you *both* dislike twins, then your opinions match," Luna pointed out logically. "And you hate to match, remember?" But of course the Shrillingbirds pretended not to hear her.

"Hello, girls! Sit, sit, sit," commanded Grandy as she pranced out of the kitchen. A giant cooking pot was tucked under her arm. Her eyes twinkled. "I thought I'd give Mac a night off from the kitchen, so I made my special Thanksgiving vegetarian stew."

"Ah, delicious!" said Grampy, rubbing his hands together.

"Ah, wonderful!" said Mac, rubbing his stomach.

The Shrillingbirds said nothing and rubbed nothing. They simply sniffed suspiciously and held out their bowls.

Luna watched and knew that something

more than stew was brewing. For one thing, Grandy only cooked on special occasions.

And it wasn't like Grandy to forgive the Shrillingbirds for napping in her bed. Or for resisting her best five-star spells.

It did not take long for Luna to figure out what twinkle-eyed Grandy was up to.

A hot-and-cold spell.

A hot-and-cold spell worked like this. Whenever the Shrillingbirds lifted their spoons to their lips, Grandy zapped the temperatures. It wasn't hard to do. In fact, Luna and Claire had learned hot-and-cold spells last summer. Just a right shoulder-roll to go from hot to cold, and a left shoulder-roll to go from cold to hot.

Grandy was rolling both her shoulders, double time.

"Is something wrong, Arianna?" Grampy asked Grandy politely.

"Not at all, Fred. I must have pulled a muscle playing golf," Grandy lied.

"Ouch, ouch, ouch!" gasped Lord Shrillingbird. "This stew is burning my mouth!"

"Ooh-ooh-ooh!" choked Lady Shrillingbird. "Whatever do you mean? It tastes like ice!"

"That's odd," said Mac, "because my stew is a perfect temperature."

"Mine, too," agreed everyone else.

Everyone except Daphne. She hardly touched her dinner. Her face dragged so low it nearly rested on the table.

Still brooding about poor popped Percival, Luna figured.

"When I move into Glenn Bly, I'm hiring a *professional* chef," said Lady Shrillingbird, throwing Grandy a dirty look and pushing away her bowl of stew. "Somebody who can prepare elegant French cuisine."

"Or Indian," said Lord Shrillingbird. "Actually, I prefer Indian cuisine."

"*I* prefer French," said Lady Shrillingbird. "*C'est magnifique.*"

"*I* prefer Indian," argued Lord Shrillingbird. Since he did not know how to say any Indian words, he thumped his fist on the table.

"May I be excused?" asked Daphne.

"I'm not feeling well."

"Certainly, dear," said Mac.

With a heavy heart, Luna watched Daphne leave the room. Poor Daphne. First an orphan. Now, maybe even homeless, thanks to them.

Grandy could cast all the silly, one-star spells she wanted, but zapping the food was not going to keep the Shrillingbirds out of Glenn Bly.

Grandy needed to be told what was really going on at this now unhaunted, but still very troubled castle.

Luna looked at Claire.

Claire looked at Luna.

Their expressions said everything.

It was time for a midnight meeting.

8
Midnight Haunting

LATER THAT EVENING, the twins sent a summons to Grandy in scrambled-letters ink, writing it on a card and slipping it under the Peacock Chamber door.

To a nonwitch, the card would nonsensically read: *I am testing the mud.*

But a witch would unscramble and rearrange the letters to find its secret message:

Meet us at midnight.

When the clock struck midnight, all three witches swiftly instaported themselves into Glenn Bly's library. The library was the best place, because witches ancient and modern have always known to meet in the room that contains the most books.

Grandy looked grim in her official robes. Around her neck hung an imposing gold medal upon which was inscribed: *Seniors Silver Loch Golf Champion.*

"Wow! Did you win that medal?" asked Claire, shocked.

"Of course not," snapped Grandy. "I spell-borrowed it for the night from Hildegarde Bruce, the *real* Seniors Silver Loch Golf champion. I thought it would be inspirational. The power of positive thinking, and all that piffle. Your grandfather and I have one more shot at the title, and I've got to feel like a champ. I also need my sleep, so you girls had better have a good reason as to why we're here." Grandy flicked her fingers so that a fire roared up in the cold hearth. "By the way, Claire, where is your robe?"

While Luna had remembered hers, and even her garnet one-and-a-half-star pin, Claire had forgotten to pack her special witch robe. So she'd had to make do with her same old Camp Bliss T-shirt over Luna's thermal long johns.

"At home," Claire mumbled. Then she quickly changed the subject. "Grandy, we've got a problem."

Quickly, she explained about the Shrillingbirds' plans to move into Glenn Bly, and how Percival should not have been popped. "So it's all a big mess," Claire concluded. "And it's kind of our fault. What should we do?"

"Yes, yes," said Grandy. "It *is* a big mess. And it's all my fault. I just didn't want to think about it until the golf tournament was over." She sat back in the armchair, cracking her knuckles. "When Mac wrote that he had a problem with ghosts, he didn't mean I should pop the one he had. He meant that he was having a problem getting more ghosts to come help haunt. He told me earlier tonight that his intention was to drive off the dratted Spillingbirds. But I couldn't bear to tell him I had popped his only ghost. And if you pop one, it's difficult to coax others over, obviously."

"So what are we going to do, Grandy?"

"Well, I don't know." Grandy scowled. "Why is it up to me to solve everything? Besides, advanced-star spells don't work on that confounding couple. Which means we can't turn them into dandelions or bread-crumb toppings or goldfish. Or, for that matter, hypnotize them into selling back Glenn Bly. Hmm. If only we knew who used to live in this castle . . ."

"Why? How would that help?" Claire leaned forward.

"Well, *obviously*," said Grandy, rolling her eyes, "if we had a record of who used to live here, we could scrounge up a really good ghost. A professional, who is specifically trained to haunt houseguests."

Claire smiled at her twin as she snapped her fingers. "I've got an idea!" She leaped out of her chair and ran to the secret, strawberry-scrolled charter-room door. "Follow me!"

With Grandy and Luna behind her, Claire led the way up-up-up the stairs, and, with a turn of the key, into the charter room.

At midnight, it was dark as the inside of a boot.

Grandy quickly took care of that. "Light, alight!" she commanded, sweeping her finger in a circle. Candles sputtered to life in their sconces. "Well, well, well," exclaimed Grandy. "What have we here?"

"See that book?" Claire pointed excitedly. "That's the Book of All Records. The whole history of Glenn Bly is in it. If you need the names of people who've lived and died at Glenn Bly, then that's the book for you!"

She pounced to the table and grabbed the quill pen. Now was her chance to sign her name. She had been itching to write *Ms. Claire Bundkin* in giant cursive letters ever since she first saw the book. She loved-loved-loved the idea of adding her name onto a thousand-year-old page of ancient history.

"Put that pen down, Claire!" hissed Luna,

snatching the quill from Claire's grasp.

"Foiled again," muttered Claire.

"Hush, girls!" said Grandy. "You're both so busy squabbling, you didn't even notice that this room is shaped like a circle!"

"Actually, I noticed," said Luna.

"And I noticed, too," said Claire.

"But. Do you know what it means?" asked Grandy.

Both twins shook their heads.

"In past centuries, circular rooms were built specially as meeting places for witches," said Grandy. "It's an outdated custom, since circle-shaped rooms proved to be such a pain in the neck to decorate. But witching power lives deep within these walls. Can't you feel it?"

Claire nodded. She did feel a bit tingly, especially in her spell-casting pinkie finger. At her side, Luna nodded, too.

Now Grandy glided over to examine the Book of All Records.

"Fascinating!" she exclaimed, as she turned the parchment pages. "Aha. Oh, yes. Very interesting."

"What's interesting, Grandy?" asked Luna.

"Well, it seems that some of these guests were actually Bramblewine witches. Sophia Spregg Bramblewine visited in 1899. And Eulalie Bramblewine was Glenn Bly's Witch Laureate in 1731. Do you know what this means, twinsicles?"

Again, the twins shook their heads.

"It means," said Grandy with a gleeful grin, "that we can cast a very BIG spell in this room, using the leftover magic of our ancient Bramblewine relatives!"

Then she cackled her special five-star cackle and clapped her hands. Claire shivered. At midnight, in her velvet robes, Grandy always seemed more frightening than she did by day in her gaucho pants and golf visor.

"Let's get to work," said Grandy. "Tonight, we'll brew up a spell more splendid than all of our stars put together. It's a once-in-a-lifetime chance. Twins, look sharp, and do what I do! I've got a plan!"

Keeping one finger held on its spine, Grandy

then sidestepped away from the Book of All Records. The twins did the same.

"*Light, blight,*" Grandy intoned.

The candles guttered and the room darkened.

"Now step counterclockwise," Grandy instructed the twins softly. "Each step will move us back one hundred years. We're walking back to 1616."

Her long robe dragged up layers of dust as she began to move backward. So did Luna's robe. Claire scuffled her feet, trying to float up some of her own dust. But since she was wearing long johns, it was basically impossible. She wished she had remembered her robe! Crumbs, she was a bad suitcase packer!

After four ponderous paces, Grandy stopped. She closed her eyes, raised her hands, and intoned:

"*Calling Bramblewines of yore,*
We borrow stars from years before."

In the pause that followed, Claire's pinkie felt extra tingly.

She checked to see if anything in the room was different. Nothing.

"No peeking!" hissed Grandy, who had also been peeking. "Eyes closed, mind open!" Then she continued:

> "Scrawny ghost of ancient castle,
> Come back, and bring your ghostly passel.
> Rescue Glenn Bly from its plight—
> Rush forward through this haunted night!

"Okay, now you can look," Grandy whispered.

Claire opened her eyes. She saw candlelit shadows on the wall tremble, then multiply, blending and crowding together as they changed shape. No longer simply reflected flames, the new silhouettes made images of heads and shoulders and arms raised high.

Claire turned, stupefied, to see that an army of ghostly knights had slowly filled the room. She recognized many faces from the tapestry of the Battle of Sodden Field. If they had been flesh-and-blood people, there would have been far too many forms to fit inside one room. But these soft phantoms simply folded, overlapped, and passed through one another.

Hundreds of them.

"Ruins and revenants!" Claire exclaimed. (*Revenant* was Claire's new word of the day. It was just a fancy word for ghost.)

"Sir Percival!" said Luna, pointing out the familiar young knight who stood proudly among the others.

Sir Percival took Luna's cry as an introduction. He nodded and then with grave ceremony stepped up onto the table.

"Speech! Speech!" cheered the ghosts, raising their swords and spears and battle-axes. Percival held his hand up for silence.

"We are here at your most powerful summons, madam," Sir Percival declared to Grandy. "We are the Knightly Order of Glenn Bly, nearly four hundred men strong!"

As the army cheered and whistled, Sir Percival dropped to his knee and bowed his head in Grandy's direction. "Good Bramblewine Witch, we are at your command!"

Claire was relieved that Percival did not seem to be holding any grudges against Grandy for that afternoon's popping.

"Well, thanks," said Grandy shyly, overwhelmed by the power of her own spell. She cleared her throat. "Then I command you to drive out the blasted Lord and Lady Screechybird! I'd have done it myself and saved you the bother, if they weren't so darn spellproof."

"No bother at all!" trumpeted Sir Percival. He spoke with extra confidence, now that he had a cheering ghost brigade at his dispatch.

"They're sleeping in our room. Elderberry Chamber," said Claire. "By the way, we'd love to get our bed back. We had to move into Humdrum Chamber, and it's damp and the ceiling drips and—"

"Men! To Elderberry Chamber!" Sir Percival commanded.

With Grandy, Claire, and Luna tagging behind, the battalion of knights lost no time stampeding down the stairs. But this was not the deafening noise one might expect. Four hundred ghosts running downstairs end up making about as much noise as distant thunder.

Still, four hundred ghosts are a lot spookier than one.

Halfway down the hall, Claire saw a small shape dart forward. She drew back with a gasp. What was that? A dog?

No, it was the same little black goat from earlier that day.

The goat had enjoyed snacking on Lord Shrillingbird's slipper so much that he had bravely tip-hoofed it back to the castle in search of the other one.

"Meh-eh-eh-eh!" bleated the goat, startled by the sudden spectacle of witches and ghosts. Sensing his opportunity, he trotted after them straight into Elderberry Chamber.

The thudding, clamorous, clanking ghosts woke up Lord and Lady Shrillingbird in an instant.

"Who goes there?" whispered Lady Shrillingbird.

"I don't see anything," said Lord Shrillingbird.

Lucky for them, Claire realized, Grandy had snapped herself and the twins with a five-minute invisibility spell.

"But don't you hear those thuds and clanks?" hissed Lady Shrillingbird, sitting up.

"*Mmph.* It's just the bad plumbing," said Lord Shrillingbird. "This castle is leaky and creaky."

"But . . . what about that icy draft?" Lady Shrillingbird shivered.

"That," said Lord Shrillingbird, "is the faulty heating."

"I think you should investigate," squeaked Lady Shrillingbird, poking her husband in the ribs. "What if it's a ghost?"

"Bah! A ghost! You've lost your last marble, my lady. I'm staying put," said Lord Shrillingbird. Though he looked as scared as his wife, Lord Shrillingbird was so used to arguing with her that he didn't know how to take her side, even at this crucial moment.

On Sir Percival's signal, some of the more playful knights began pulling on the curtains. A few others used all of their phantom might to rattle the windowpanes. And one daring young foot soldier started jumping on the edge of the Shrillingbirds' bed, causing the springs to squeak slightly.

"Wow. This is even better than the Chain Chant spell," Claire whispered to Luna. "These ghost guys are professionals!"

"Better than an ogre!" Luna whispered back.

By now, both Shrillingbirds looked terrified.

"I'm frightened!" peeped Lady Shrillingbird.

"I'm not!" But Lord Shrillingbird pulled up the covers and pressed his hands over his ears.

"Fool, you're only saying that to be stubborn!" hissed Lady Shrillingbird. "I know a haunt when I hear it, and this castle's got ghosts!" She hopped out of bed and began nervously running back and forth. "We'd better dash. Oh, how dreadful! We'll never even be able to sell it, not with a ghost ruining its market value. Hurry, my lord. Time to bolt!"

"I'm not scared, and I don't feel like dashing or bolting," said Lord Shrillingbird disagreeably. Then he pretended to be relaxed by stretching his hands behind his head and wriggling his toes.

When the goat caught sight of all those delicious-looking, wriggling toes—almost as good as a slipper—he took hold of one and gave it a gentle nibble.

"Argh!" Lord Shrillingbird jumped out of bed and flung himself into Lady Shrillingbird's arms. "The ghost just bit me!"

"Dimwit! Ghosts don't bite!" said Lady Shrillingbird, smirking.

"Sometimes they do!"

"Do not!"

"Do so—argh!" Lord Shrillingbird yelped as the goat nipped for a taste of his ankle. "I think I might, actually . . . agree with you, my lady. Perhaps we ought to get out of here!"

So Lady Shrillingbird grabbed her purse, then hoisted Lord Shrillingbird up and over her shoulder like a sack of grain. Then she ran for it, speeding down the hall and taking the stairs three at a time.

"Whoa. Lady Shrill sure can move," whispered Claire. "She'd win relays at Tower Hill Middle, easy."

Grandy, the twins, the ghosts, and the goat followed hard on the Shrillingbirds' heels. They tailed them through Glenn Bly's iron-hinged doors and all the way down the lawn, to where the Rolls-Royce was parked.

"We're safe, we're free!" squealed Lady Shrillingbird. "Safe and free!" She swung open the car door and tossed her husband in the back.

"Step on it!" yelped Lord Shrillingbird.

Lady Shrillingbird hopped in the driver's seat and revved the engine. With a screech of tires, the Shrillingbirds' car plowed across the lawn and disappeared down the hill and into the darkness.

"*Adios*, creeps!" called Claire.

The goat bleated agreement. Lord Shrillingbird's toes had left a terrible, crumbled-cheese aftertaste.

"They're better off in the city, anyway," declared Luna. "There's more stuff to complain about in cities."

Grandy yawned. "Twins, you'll catch cold if you stay outside too long. It's your life, but I'd get back to bed. And thank you, Sir Percival," she added, with a nod to the knight, "for a job well done."

Then she snapped her fingers and vanished into the mist.

"A three-star spell," murmured Claire. "Crumbs, I wish I knew how to do it. Well, maybe next year."

"What a lovely night," said Sir Percival.

Claire looked up. The knight was right. It was cold and beautiful. A full moon hung in the navy blue sky. The silvery moonlight and the silvery light of the ghostly knights shone softly over the meadow.

But something strange was happening.

"Look around, Clairsie," said Luna. "The ghosts are fading."

Sure enough, right before Claire's eyes, the

ghosts were beginning to curl up along their edges. The faint popping as each departed— *plip blip plip*—sounded like a thousand bath bubbles were escaping into the air.

"Where are they going?" wondered Claire.

"Off to haunt another needy castle?" suggested Luna.

Together, the twins watched the misty veil that sparkled in the air after the ghost knights were gone. Now the night was rich with a faint but sweet and lingering scent. Claire sniffed, then inhaled deeply. What was that delicious smell?

Then she knew.

Strawberries.

And then all at once, a heavy mass of clouds swept across the clear sky, hiding the moon and stars.

"Oh, no, not again!" wailed Luna. "Here comes the rain!"

9
Strawberry Birthday Surprise

WHEN LUNA WOKE UP the next morning, she could feel the difference immediately. Maybe it was on account of her witch-smarts, or maybe it was because she was a light sleeper. But something about Glenn Bly seemed a little bit less creaky and a little bit more cheery.

She leaped out of bed and ran directly to the window. What she saw outside made her smile with delight.

Instead of a brown and wintry lawn, her eyes were dazzled by a field of blazing green.

"Claire!" she cried. "Come look!"

"Wha . . . ?" Her sister rolled out from under the quilts and crept up sleepily behind her to see. "Thickets and thistledown! It's like summertime in November!" exclaimed Claire. "Now, here's the Scotland I always wanted!"

"Clairsie, I think what we're looking at is a giant strawberry patch," speculated Luna. "It's right at the exact same place where all the ghosts popped." She put her hands to her heart. "How romantic. The brave knights gave us something to remember them by."

"Well, I'm remembering that I'm hungry. Let's go get some strawberries for breakfast!" said Claire, pulling on her rainbow-sleeves jacket.

Together, the twins flew out into the cold morning, which was filled with summertime smells. They plomped right down in the middle of the strawberry patch, and soon were feasting on the biggest, juiciest, most divine wild strawberries they'd ever tasted in their lives.

"Mmm-mmm. Even if we didn't end up with half-stars for driving out the Shrillingbirds, these strawberries were worth the effort," said Claire, sitting back to wipe her strawberry-stained hands on the grass.

"Hey, here comes Daphne." Luna pointed just as Daphne rode up on a shiny blue bicycle with a straw handlebar basket.

When Daphne saw the strawberries, she nearly fell off her seat. "We have to tell Grandpop!" she exclaimed. "Or better yet, let's show him. Hurry, help me fill this basket!"

Quickly, they picked strawberries until Daphne's basket was full. When they called Mac down to the kitchen and presented the basket, then pointed out toward the field, his eyes filled with wonder.

"I don't believe it. Strawberries haven't grown on this field since the terrible Battle of Sodden Field," he said. "But I don't understand. How could a field of strawberries just grow up overnight?"

Luna shrugged. "Mysterious things happen

a lot in Scotland," she said.

Mac pronged a berry between his thumb and finger. "With all-season strawberries, I suppose we'll have plenty of visitors wanting to spend a weekend at our bed-and-breakfast. And that means perhaps we'll be able to purchase Glenn Bly back from the Shrillingbirds," he said. His eyes glowed with future plans and prospects. "And then we'll turn some of this land into a public park, for people to visit. Would you like that, Daphne?"

"Like it?" Daphne jumped up and down. "I couldn't think of a better birthday present!"

Then everyone felt terrible, because in all the excitement they had forgotten that today was Daphne's birthday. Everyone, that is, except for Mac, who had given her the new blue bicycle earlier that morning.

"Crumbs, we don't even have any gifts for her," Luna whispered behind her hand to her twin.

Luckily, when Grandy and Grampy came home later (after placing second-to-last in the golf tournament) they were able to wrap up a couple of items from the Silver Loch Pro Shop that they had been planning to give Justin.

"Not that a golf umbrella and three pairs of athletic socks are the greatest gift, but I guess they're better than nothing," said Luna.

"Yeah, and thank goodness for those strawberries," said Claire, "otherwise Daphne wouldn't have had a very good birthday from us, gifts-wise."

It didn't take long for the word of the magical strawberries to spread. By afternoon, the people who lived on the surrounding farms and towns had come to witness the magical strawberry field. While some onlookers clicked pictures, others sampled the berries.

Afterward, Mac invited everyone into the castle kitchen, where he blew the dust off an ancient Glenn Bly cookbook, *Four Score and Twenty Recipes for Strawberries*, and made a giant, gooey, gorgeous strawberry birthday cake.

"By the way, where are the Shrillingbirds?" asked Grampy.

"They might be halfway to Baja by now," said Grandy. "And Mac, I don't think you'll have a problem buying back your castle. I have a hunch those two won't be visiting here anytime soon."

"And why do I have a feeling your special charms did the trick, Arianna?" asked Mac with a warm wink. "You are one of my favorite problem solvers."

Grandy smiled back. "I do what I can," she said, batting her eyelashes.

"Oh, I can't wait to be old and have old flames," said Luna.

"Harrumph. I can't wait to be old and hog all the credit for stuff," said Claire.

When the twins went looking for Sir Percival, they found him in his usual place, behind the clock on the landing.

"I knew it!" exclaimed Luna. "I knew you wouldn't stay popped for long."

"Not a chance. I'm this castle's guardian ghost," he explained. "I'm here to protect Glenn Bly forever." He jingled his amulet proudly. He looked a little bit bolder after last night's stunning victory over the Shrillingbirds.

"If you ever need help guarding," said Claire, "you can call on us,"

The final night at Glenn Bly was the best yet. In honor of Daphne's birthday, the Bundkins, Blys, and Bramblewines stayed up late playing five-card poker and charades. Afterward, Mac taught them a Scottish reel.

"The best things about the Shrillingbirds being vamoosed is that we get our beds back," said Claire when the twins went upstairs to bed. "Humdrum Chamber was the pits."

But as they settled into bed, thunder rumbled in the distance.

"Storm number four!" Claire's eyes widened.

"I guess the rain helps the strawberries grow," yawned Luna.

The goat, who had moved into Elderberry Chamber on account of its tasty armchair cushions, bleated in agreement.

The next morning, it was time to bid goodbye to Glenn Bly, and everyone was slightly sad, except for Grampy, who had not warmed to old flame Mac, and had not enjoyed being humiliated on the golf course.

On the other hand, Daphne seemed saddest of all.

"You'll come back in the summer, right?" asked Daphne. "In the summer, it never gets dark here. It stays twilight all through the night." She turned to Claire. "Did you know that, American Claire?"

"Nope," said Claire. "But did you know that *crepuscular* is another word for twilight?"

"Nope," said Daphne. "I wonder, which of us has the most interesting fact?"

They both looked at Luna to be tiebreaker.

"Daphne," said Luna, decisively. And though she hoped to visit Daphne Bly again, she was glad she would be able to stop breaking ties for a while.

With only a few minutes until their plane landed in Philadelphia, the twins shook Luna's spy globe to see what was happening in other parts of their world. The colors of the globe swirled like a sunlit summer stream as they passed it back and forth.

"Show us Glenn Bly," commanded Luna.

Inside the globe, a picture of the castle focused. Mac and Daphne were both in the stable, feeding the horses.

"And not a Shrillingbird in sight," Luna noted contentedly.

"Show us our family," said Claire, fogging the glass.

Now an image of their mom, Steve, Justin, their dad, Fluffy, and baby Bert appeared. They were all sitting together in the airport, waiting for the plane to get in. (Well, Justin wasn't sitting. He was playing Hacky Sack.)

"Crumbs, our family keeps getting bigger and bigger!" said Luna.

"And better and better," added Claire. "Hey, Loon, what were your favorite parts of our visit to Glenn Bly?"

"Tea in the drawing room, exploring the castle with Daphne, and learning how to make strawberry scones and cake," Luna answered promptly. "What were yours?"

"Riding Dooley, chasing out the Shrilling-birds, and sneaking into the Charter Room early this morning to write my name in the Book of All Records," said Claire.

The twins grinned at each other. Opposites forever.

"What about me?" their grandmother called softly across the aisle so that she didn't wake up Grampy. "Aren't you going to ask me my favorite part of the trip?"

"What were your favorite parts?" the twins asked Grandy together.

"That's easy." Grandy smiled. "Playing golf with Fred and listening to those terrific thunderstorms as I fell asleep!"

Then she tossed a honey-roasted peanut in the air and caught it in her mouth.

"Crumbs, those thunderstorms kept me awake, Grandy," said Luna.

"Yeah, I thought they were totally spooky," said Claire.

"Nonsense. Nothing says Scotland to me

better than a good loud rain. It really sets the mood."

"Wait a minute, Grandy. Were *you* the one casting spells to make all that stormy weather?" Luna leaned forward, indignant, to catch her grandmother's eye.

"Of course I was. To me, a good thunderstorm is like a little lullaby," Grandy answered, settling back in her seat and adjusting the mini pillow at her neck. "And as the saying goes, 'Into every life, a noisy storm must thunder.'"

And although Luna had a feeling this was not quite the right saying, it sounded perfectly true when Grandy said it. Which was always the case.